# Driftwood from the Specific

## A genre-hopping collection

By

A.P. Gilbert

© 2014 Anthony Paul Gilbert

All rights reserved. This book or any portion thereof
may not be reproduced or used in any manner whatsoever
without the express written permission of the author
except for the use of brief quotations in a book review.

ISBN-13:
978-1499537550

ISBN-10:
1499537557

http://tonygilbertauthor.weebly.com/

Thank you so much for purchasing my book. I hope that you find something within its pages that you enjoy.

Before you begin, I would like to draw your attention to a few people who have made this work possible. Rather than bore you with the details, I will just provide you with a short list.

My wife, for putting up with my evenings of silence.

Leyland Perree for the title.

Joseph Murphy for the cover.

Alex S. Johnson for the audio version.

All of my beta readers – too many to mention.

Special thanks to Paul Gilbert and Julie Sibley for their editing skills.

To you, my readers, the people who keep me writing.

Thank you all.

Cover design by M Joseph Murphy.

http://MJosephMurphy.info

using an image from Konfusion-Design (deviantart)

## A Breath of Fresh Air

"It's a good turnout, George"

"Yup."

The two old friends looked across at the gathering of people, all standing in their own little groups, most engaged in muted conversation.

"Did you expect it?"

"Nah, not this many."

"I wasn't talking about them."

"Oh," he said, running his fingers along the short grey stubble of his chin, enjoying the feeling on his fingertips. "That."

He didn't elaborate on his response, he didn't need to. His lack of answer told his friend all he needed to know.

A light pattering of rain began to fall, drumming softly against the deep green leaves overhead. The groups of people, each mimicking the other, looked towards the heavens and began the short stroll back to their cars. George watched as they walked then smiled as a young girl turned to look at him before being whisked into the arms of a man he knew to be her dad.

"Go on," his friend said gently, with a nod of his head.

George followed his gaze towards the last remaining figure, the one with raindrops glistening in her short black hair. He pushed himself up from the stone bench, hands on knees, and realised he no longer had to struggle up; he felt better than he had in years.

She didn't turn around as he approached. She didn't turn as he put his hand on her shoulder, nor when he spoke her name.

"Hilda."

Her eyes were red and puffy, her cheeks stained with tears, but to George she still looked as beautiful as she ever had. Hilda fell to her knees upon the damp grass as a fresh wave of sobs spilled from her sad green eyes.

Please don't cry, George went to say but was interrupted by a man in a smart black suit, sunglasses fixed across the bridge of a perfectly straight nose; George's son.

"C'mon Mum," he said, helping her tenderly to her feet.

There were so many things that he wanted to say to them both, but could only watch now, as they walked away. His eyes followed them as mother and son entered the awaiting car and pulled away, the sound of tyres on gravel reverberating through the empty graveyard. He turned around and traced the words inscribed into the grey stone cross.

George Theobald Harris

8th Feb 1922 – 23rd Apr 2003

Husband, Father, Grandfather

Loved And Missed By All

"It's time to go," George's old friend said, interrupting his musings.

"But I'm not done; I still have things to do."

"Most people say the same thing."

His old friend took his hand in his own and a pleasant warmth spread through him. He led him across the grounds, weaving between gravestones, old and new.

"Where are we going?"

"You said it yourself, George. You still have things to do."

George looked back over his shoulder at the car as it disappeared into the thickening traffic of the late afternoon.

"Not with them though," his friend said, pulling George's concentration back. "There is another family waiting your arrival."

"Sorry?" George asked, confused. "What do you mean?"

"South Dakota, a small town called Hazel."

"I don't understand."

"A nice family, your mother's name is Jennifer."

"My mother's name is Anita!" George almost shouted, but his companion just nodded. "Who are you?"

The man, who looked like his old friend smiled, and George's anger dissipated almost instantly.

"I am known by many names."

"What can I call you?" George asked carefully.

"I'll tell you next time," he said, his blue eyes sparkling.

"Next time?" he asked, but the man was gone and all was black.

+++

"Where am I?" George thought, more than said.

He was cramped up in a space little bigger than himself. He felt around with limbs which didn't quite seem to be his own. He could hear distant voices, and louder screams. A calm voice spoke but as soon as the words reached him, they were forgotten. An increase in pressure gripped him and pushed him downwards, head first. More voices, more sounds. Then, bright light hurting his eyes. He closed them and hands grasped his head, tugging him forcefully from warm wetness into cold air. That's when he began to scream.

Jennifer lay back against the white plastic pillow as her new baby was put to her breast.

"Is he okay?" she asked, still breathless, her hair plastered against the side of her moist, reddened face.

"He's fine," the midwife smiled. "I'll leave you three alone. Happy birthday little one."

## Warm Wishes

"It's Christmas," Andy whispered to his brother, Philip. It was still early and he tried hard to focus as he looked with happy anticipation at the five year old sitting up in the bed opposite his own.

"Do you think he has been?"

"Of course he's been!" Andy smiled at his brother, who was four years his junior; he was so naïve it was funny. "Father Christmas comes every year."

"Can we go downstairs then?"

"Okay, but we've got to be quiet, Mummy and Daddy might not be awake yet."

"Okay."

Philip and Andy slowly pulled back the covers of their beds and stepped softly onto the carpeted floor of the bedroom they shared. By now, both of their eyes had become accustomed to the poor light and they crept to the door, being careful to avoid the toys that they had left on the floor the day before. Philip bent before they reached the door and picked up his favourite bear, Bob Bear, and held it by the paw.

"I'm cold," Philip said, a little too loudly.

Andy put his finger to his lips and made a shushing sound which sounded louder than Philip's small voice. "Put your dressing gown on then."

Andy took Philip's Spiderman dressing gown from the hook on the wall and passed it over to his brother before putting his own blue one on. They tiptoed to the door and Andy opened it, being careful not to pull too quickly for fear that the bell decoration that hung on the handle would ring. It didn't and they walked out to the hall and to the top of the stairs. Looking down, Philip saw that the lights carefully wrapped around the tree were still twinkling, sending coloured flashes of red and green onto the wall of the stairway. They began to creep down. There was a breeze coming from somewhere that brushed bare ankles beneath their gowns as they reached the middle of the stairs. The brothers were both too excited to pay much mind to it but Andy did find himself pulling his dressing gown tighter around his small frame.

The two brothers reached the foot of the stairs and Philip grabbed Andy's hand in excitement at the sight of the treats that had been deposited beneath the tree. Boxes and packages of all shapes and sizes surrounded it, all wrapped in bright coloured paper and shiny ribbons. The fireplace behind the tree still held glowing embers from the night before and four fur-rimmed red stockings hung from the mantelpiece above. The stockings were packed full of gifts, nearly spilling over onto the hearth beneath. On top of the mantelpiece was the plate of cookies; half eaten, and the half glass of whisky that he and Philip had left out for Father Christmas the night before. Philip saw that half of the dog treat that he had left out for the reindeers had fallen on to the cream carpet beneath.

"Where's Lucky, Andy?" Philip asked realising that the family Labrador had not done his normal friendly attack as soon as the children came downstairs.

"I don't know," said Andy, looking around confusedly and walking towards the kitchen. It was then that he noticed the front door was open. "Mum!" he shouted, "Lucky has run away!"

Tears sprang instantly to Philips eyes and he began to sob quietly. Andy rushed past him and started up the stairs.

"Mum! Dad!" he shouted and Philip followed his lead, calling between small sobs.

"Mummy!"

Andy had already reached the top of the stairs before Philip had climbed half way and he burst in to his parents' room.

"Mum! Dad! Lucky has run away!"

There was no movement from beneath the covers and Andy rushed around to his mum's side of the bed as Philip reached the doorway. Andy pulled back the cover, expecting to see his mum's sleeping face, but she wasn't there. He pulled the cover firmly down, uncovering the side of the bed where his dad always slept.

"Philip, turn the light on," he said in a shaky voice.

"Daddy won't be happy," he said, his sobs more under control now.

"TURN THE LIGHT ON!"

Philip did and they both looked at the empty bed and then at each other. Philip's moans started up again with more vigour and tears began to well up in Andy's eyes.

Andy pushed past his brother and checked the bathroom but the light was off and the room was empty.

"Are they outside, Andy?"

"How am I supposed to know?" he said, his voice betraying the fear he now felt, and Philip started to cry harder. So, taking on his big brother role he said, with more courage than he felt, "Let's go and look."

They walked downstairs, hand in hand, slower than they had ascended, the dark of the living room seeming more ominous now, despite and perhaps because of the still flickering lights on the tree. They reached the bottom and Andy clicked on the main light, showering the room in a yellow glow and taking away the magical look of Christmas morning that they had loved when they'd first come down. They walked through into the kitchen, Philip walking slightly behind his brother but still gripping his hand tightly. They both looked at the open door at the end of the short corridor and into the forbidding darkness outside.

"You stay here," Andy said to his younger brother, pulling his hand from Philip's grip.

"I don't want to," Philip said between sobs.

"Look, I'll only be there." Andy pointed at the door. He must have sounded braver than he felt because Philip offered a small nod and pulled Bob Bear to his tiny chest.

Andy started walking towards the front door, fear sitting deep in the pit of his stomach, butterflies flapping around uncontrollably.

The cold had begun to seep in, causing goose bumps to raise on his skin as a shiver went down his spine.

"Lucky!" Philip's happy call made Andy twist round and look.

Philip was down on his knees facing the wall.

"Here boy," he said, pinching his fingers together, feigning the presence of food. "What's the matter boy? It's me, Philip." Philip turned his head to see Andy looking from the kitchen doorway.

Lucky stood beneath the kitchen table looking at each of the boys in turn, his hackles raised and a low deep growl rumbling from his closed lips.

"What's the matter boy," Andy joined in but Lucky did not stop his growl and would not approach them.

Philip started to shuffle along on his knees, edging closer to the dog but Lucky's lips curled up, baring his teeth. Andy pulled his brother back by his shoulders in alarm.

"There's something wrong with him," he said.

"What?"

Just then, the brothers heard a scream from outside and they both looked at each other, simultaneously recognising the voice of their Mum somewhere in that horrible sound. Andy ran towards the door as Philip jumped to his feet and followed, leaving Bob Bear alone on the floor.

They called her name over and over until, before stepping over the threshold into the black cold, they saw her across the way. She was standing on the street in their Dad's arms, surrounded by people from their road. Mrs Millings from next door was there and Jamie from across the road. There were other people too and Andy recognised them all but he was too preoccupied with his Dad, who was staring at the house, ignoring his brother and him and their increasingly anguished calls.

"Dad!" he screamed and Philip shouted the same but not one person looked towards them.

"Andy, your…"

Andy swivelled round and they both screamed as they saw each other at the same time. Their clothes had gone, just patches left, welded to red and blistering skin. Clumps of hair smouldered on top of their heads. Flames flew out all around them, licking their blackening skin, but they felt nothing. Lucky cowered beneath the burning table and shrunk down to his haunches as something upstairs exploded with a furious bang, shaking the ground and sending the ceiling directly above their heads crashing down.

+++

Philip shot up in his bed a scream in his throat and Andy sat looking at him.

"It's Christmas!" the older boy whispered, looking slightly shocked at his brothers' abrupt awakening.

Philip looked around the room and then smiled, *only a dream*. He shivered slightly before leaning over and pulling a small wrapped gift from beneath his bed. He passed it to his big brother who instantly began tearing at the paper.

"Thank you!" he cawed, looking at the action figure he held in front of him.

He leapt out of bed and over to his brother, hugging him, a joyous grin spread across his face but Philip did not return the hug. He was staring too intently at the charred black and twisted figurine which Andy had thrown onto his bed.

Andy pulled away, his face close to Philips. "What's wrong?"

The smell of smoke was on his breath.

**Bonfire Boy**

Here I am sitting

By my pale blue mitten

And I feel alone

So alone

So alone


My father's been weeping

While mother's been sleeping

His weakness unknown

It's not shown

It's not shown

The birds ceased their singing

Church bells gave up ringing

And all sound is silent

It's gone

Oh, it's gone


The dark day has risen

The flame's now my prison

Of dust and of ashes

Above me

They lay

## **The Daily Grind**

"I've got that interview tomorrow, honey."

"Oh yeah, I forgot about that. I'll take the bus, save you having to worry about walking to the bus stop."

"Perfect, thanks, hun."

The next morning I found myself up with the morning chorus. This interview was the one that I had been waiting for since I left university. I'd had other jobs of course, but this one could be the big one. My suit, cleaned and pressed, was hanging on the back of the door in the bedroom that I shared with my girlfriend, Jenny. I stroked it as I walked past on the way towards the kitchen of our one bedroom apartment. I fixed myself a light breakfast, pondering questions that I may be asked later on in the day.

So, what will you bring to the role? Well, I have lots of good ideas that I believe will aid—

The bread jumped from the toaster, so I buttered it thickly before sitting down to read the job description for the hundredth time this week.

"Morning, handsome."

"Morning, beautiful."

Jenny had just emerged from the shower. She was elegant in just a towel, droplets of water glistened on pale white skin. I had to tear my eyes away; focus, focus!

"How are you feeling, babe?"

"I'm good, thanks."

I was feeling good; she bent down and gave me a kiss on the cheek.

"Just remember, be yourself."

"I'll try."

"And if you don't get it—"

"I know, it's not the end of the world."

"Exactly. There will be other interviews."

"Uh huh."

"Just be yourself."

"Will do."

I didn't eat my toast.

After several trips to the toilet and a long, hot shower (interrupted briefly by Jen with 'good luck' and a kiss) my nerves had almost abated, although there were still a few butterflies in my stomach flittering around nonchalantly.

I delicately knotted my deep blue tie into a half Windsor before feeding my arms into my suit jacket. It fit me perfectly, wanting to be worn. I stood in front of Jenny's full length mirror, checking my tie again and the lay of my hair. Then, taking a deep breath, I took my briefcase from the floor of the hall. My car keys hung above the telephone table as always, so I took them and walked out, locking the door behind me.

I sat down in the front seat of my Ford KA Sport and lay my briefcase next to me. As I turned my satellite navigation on and chose the pre-planned destination, I silently ran through a checklist of things I knew about the company I was interviewing for. I think I had everything covered; I put my keys into the ignition.

The engine turned over, and over, and over. I pressed my foot to the floor, turning the key again, squeezing the steering wheel in hope, nails digging into the soft leather. No go.

"It's a test. That's what it is, a test."

I looked at the clock, it was early. I got out, grabbed my things and headed in the direction of the bus stop. I still felt good but I was grinding my teeth.

The bus stop was only a short walk away and the buses ran regularly (if I remembered correctly from my college days) yet I walked briskly, eager to get back on track.

There were four other people at the bus stop; an elderly lady with mad purple hair, permed to within an inch of its life; a young (and no doubt single) mum with a sleeping baby in a filthy looking buggy; and Mr Durgan, my next door neighbour, I nodded at him in greeting. The bus pulled up five minutes after I arrived; thank god for small mercies. I stood at the back of the queue, willing everyone to get on quickly. It was just starting to rain.

"£1.40 please."

I reached into my pocket, realising when I was half way there that my wallet was still on the nightstand.

"No fare, no travel, I'm afraid."

I ground my teeth and my hands worked on imaginary stress balls as I willed the money to magically appear.

"I'll pay."

Mr Durgan; my neighbour; my friend; my saviour!

"Thank you so much."

The other passengers; who ranged in age from 2 weeks old to 200 years old by the look of some of the old wrinklies; all went back to looking at their laps as I walked to an empty seat. The bus set off as the rain (as is customary for an English summer) began to drive down in black sheets onto the windshield. I still had plenty of time to get to my interview, so I closed my eyes and calmed down.

Meditation works in many ways; it aids creativity; it relieves stress; it helps with focus and concentration; to build self-confidence…

"Last stop."

… to increase a sense of…

"Oh for goodness sake!!!"

I ran from the bus' open doors into a tropical storm; discarded rubbish sailed past on stormy seas.

I should have asked for directions before I ran from the bus, because as I looked around I didn't recognise a thing. I ground my teeth; I was beginning to get lockjaw.

When I was a child I loved walking in the rain but as an adult, not as much fun as I remember. It's cold, it's wet and in smart shoes it becomes very slippery.

I ran into a nearby department store to get out of the rain and asked the first person I saw for directions.

"If you walk to the entrance on the far side of the store, you'll see it across the road."

Relieved, I looked at my watch and saw that I still had half an hour before I needed to be there. I decided to neaten myself up so I headed towards the bathrooms on the third floor.

I would likely have to remove most of my clothes so I went into the disabled toilet, not looking around before I walked through the door, knowing there would be at least one person staring at me, wondering what my disability was. I put on a limp, just in case.

I spent the next ten minutes frantically wringing out my clothes into the tiny sink and drying them as best I could using a hand dryer with less puff than a ninety year old smoker. I removed my shoes and poured away the murky pools. My socks went in the bin after an attempt at ridding them of water led to my hands being stained a pale blue. So, looking like an extra from Avatar, I pulled my damp clothes back on and squeezed my feet uncomfortably into my loafers. I briefly checked my tie and my dripping hair in the mirror before picking up my briefcase and heading for the door. I twisted the handle and it came off in my hand.

"You have got to be kidding me!"

I threw my briefcase across the floor, where it clattered noisily into the bin and I hammered at the door with both fists. My shouts echoed around the tiled walls, but obviously no further because no one came to my aid. I tried running at it but managed only to hurt my shoulder. I tried to get my well bitten fingernails into the gap between door and frame but succeeded only in grunting through grinding teeth. I slumped down to the floor with a lump in the back of my throat. I felt like sobbing when I looked at my watch to see that I had five minutes left. It was then that I noticed the red emergency pull cord dangling next to the toilet bowl. Scrambling to my feet I dived at it and pulled; a dying man's last hope.

The door opened nearly seven minutes later and I sprinted from the room, snatching my briefcase from the floor as I did.

"Out of the way."

I ran down the aisles towards the exit, not caring who I pushed or insulted. I could see the glass doors in the distance, and through them, my salvation. I was late, I knew that, but I was going to get there. The automatic door opened just in time and I sped into the street. The rain had stopped, the sun now high and strong. Cigarette smoke met my nostrils as I weaved between honking vehicles, my eyes set on my goal.

"Hello, I'm a little late I'm afraid. I have an interview with Mr Dennison."

The middle aged woman behind the desk stared at me through wire rimmed spectacles.

"Name?"

"John Nesbitt."

She scanned her little green book with one long finger and then turned the page. She looked up at me again and with just a tiny hint of humour in her voice, she spoke.

"Mr Nesbitt, your interview is tomorrow."

## An Ode to Art

I hate it when they scream.

It reeks of narcissism.

I tell them time after time that it is not about them but they refuse to listen to reason. Even after I remove their tongues, their incessant noises continue to interrupt my art.

My work is well known in the field, though very few know my medium, nor my subjects. They call it modern art; I call it mimesis. For, what better definition is there for human behaviour in art than the transition between life and death?

Death. It has a sound that I enjoy and it ends with a serpents kiss. Dying, on the other hand is an unusual word. It is defined as the time when something ends. Dying, though, is my life and as the light fades from my subjects eyes I know that they recognise the continuation of their life appearing on the canvas before them.

I used to paint twice a year but the want, no, the need to create more exquisite pieces has driven me forward and even now, minutes after the completion of Michelle #9, I can hear my muse knocking at the door. I think I shall call my next work, You.

# How to write a poem

I have had plenty of chats,
With guys in gloves and girls in hats,
About whether poems should rhyme,
So if you're kind and have the time,
I'd love to have your thoughts on this,
But please don't snarl or bite or hiss.

        A poem
    doesn't have to
                  rhyme
      as long
        as
        it's
spread around the page
        ran
     domly.

I have tried and I have failed,
I've given up, I've run, I've bailed,
Non rhyming poems can(?) make sense,
And arguments can be intense.

Now, listen to this -
What if I finish a line with the word orange?
Or silver?
Or antidisestablishmentarianism?
Do I have to end the verse by rhyming it with prism?

                                  If you want
                 to write a poem
                        that
                  doesn't rhyme,
                  write
                                          a
                  book!

Please be aware that all the views expressed here
Are not necessarily my own
But if you'd like to rhyme with me
I'm always on the phone!

# Blink

The first one appeared under his right arm. Small, disguised by the mass of dark hair that grew there. Just a black line, a hole, no more than three quarters of an inch in length. David thought it was just a hair at first, hardened by his roll on deodorant. He scratched at it to try and soften it but to his obvious disgust, the tip of his finger slipped in. David let out a small yip and took a step back.

"Whoa, what the hell?"

There was no pain, just a strange pressure as his finger stretched the tiny hole. He lifted his arm above his head and walked over to the bathroom mirror to get a closer look. It didn't look like an injury, could have been a simple black biro mark if he hadn't known any better. There was no redness or inflamed skin, just a line. Then it moved. Just a small movement. David would have missed it if he hadn't been staring straight at it. It had moved, almost like a fishes gill. No, more like a blink. David let his arm drop and rubbed his eyes.

"I definitely need more sleep" he said and let out a small, slightly nervous sigh.

Tiredness can do that to a person; make them see things, believe things that cannot possibly be real.

David turned to the small cubicle behind him and turned the shower on. As the water poured out he walked from the small bathroom to grab the towel, still damp, from its place on his bedroom floor. His mobile barked from the table next to his bed. A text message from his girlfriend; what time are you getting here this morning? David opened up the small touchscreen keypad and typed his reply. When he walked back into the bathroom, the steam had clouded the mirror, his fingerprints visible along the edge.

David hopped under the shower, his skin reddening almost immediately under the hot flow. He washed quickly, remembering the promise to his girlfriend; he needed to be out of the door in about 10 minutes. By the time he had got out, realised he had left his towel in the bedroom, dripped all over the floor, slipped and stubbed his toe, got dried and dressed and left the house, he had forgotten all about the line under his arm.

+++

David didn't emerge from his bed until gone 11, after a light and broken sleep. Charlotte had left at 6 for work but he had no work today. It had been a good evening. They had watched a romantic comedy at the Odeon; which seemed as funny and romantic as every other romantic comedy released in the last ten years. This had been followed by dinner and drinks, then home so Charlotte could say 'thank you'.

David walked into the small kitchen/diner and turned on the TV. There was a cartoon playing. He yawned and stretched, remembering last night. They had never filmed it before; it had been Charlotte's idea. She had made him promise not to watch it before she got back from work. David thought about this. She would never know, and "what she doesn't know won't hurt her".

David went into the bedroom and ejected the disk from the digital camera at the foot of the bed. He only had a 14 inch combi in his room so strode purposefully into the living room to make full use of the 52" HD TV, blue ray player and Bose surround sound system. The curtains were still drawn, a small sliver of light came through in-between them separating the room into two unequal sides and causing a reflection on the TV. David walked over and pulled the curtains together. The light disappeared. He sat down, master controller in his left hand and watched. It was all looking good, both of them had better than average bodies, Charlotte had a fantastic bum. It was about ten minutes in when David had needed to stop the disk, skip it back and watch it again.

He had already removed Charlottes top and had his arms above his head while she slipped off his. It was once his armpit was revealed that caused him to sharply intake a breath. He had forgotten all about the line under his arm. He held his hand over his mouth, his index finger resting against his top lip. The line was still there, and not only was it longer and wider, there was now something protruding from it.

"What the hell is that?" David put his hand up his T-shirt sleeve and tentatively felt the hair under his arm. There it was, not large, about 2 inches from the line to the tip, and hard. A trip to the doctors was in order. Grabbing his trousers and his car keys he left the apartment at a jog.

David arrived home at just after 3pm. It had been a wasted trip. It was only a short drive and as he travelled he had phoned for an emergency appointment. He arrived, checked in and walked into a room so full of snot filled, coughing kids that he had to stand back outside again. It was loud and warm, there was no air conditioning and the small window on the far side of the room was only open an inch. People were called out of the waiting room by the doctors on duty and other people arrived with paper white children wrapped in their arms. Kids argued and shouted at each other and David had begun to get a headache.

He left the vicinity of the waiting room, walking down the narrow stairs and outside to get some air. It was warm for September and there were no clouds to shield the early afternoon sun. It was still cooler out here than in the waiting room which was surely a breeding place for sickness. Why is it that doctors never seem to get ill? David had absently checked his arm pit again, through his T-shirt, feeling a light sweat but no lump. It didn't take much persuading to stop him from going back in. He had headed back home.

His phone rang. David walked over to the small table next to the front door where he had left it along with his car keys and the half-drunk bottle of Evian he had bought on the way back. 'Charlotte Work' was displayed on the large screen. The words disappeared before he could answer it.

He unlocked his phone and dialled the number back, but was met with the familiar 'beep beep beep' of a phone in use. Walking back down the short hall towards the living room he noticed something on the light cream carpet right next to the skirting board. He bent to his knees and looked closer at his find. It would have seemed fairly insignificant if in the right area but it was completely out of place.

It grew from the carpet. David picked it up, one tiny root snapped with an audible pop. A translucent stem split about 1cm from the root into two small, round green leaves. David stood, rolling the stem in between his index finger and thumb. The leaves were solid but soft to the touch and they let out a small amount of clear liquid onto his palm as he pushed his thumbnail into it. David walked into the living room and left into the kitchen/diner, dropping the weed into the bin.

He filled and began to boil the kettle while checking the voicemail which had appeared as a message on his phone. It was from Charlotte; she wasn't going to make it round tonight, too much work on, and don't watch the video without her. "Sorry babe" thought David, "too late, but not to worry, don't think I'll be watching the rest!"

He turned off the kettle and opened the fridge, pulling out a Bud before heading into the living room and jumping onto the sofa. He turned the TV on, flicked through the channels until he found a violent action movie and promptly, surprisingly fell asleep.

He knew he was dreaming because Charlotte was there but she didn't look like Charlotte. It was just the two of them, walking down a paved, walled in alleyway. Everything was right angles, nothing out of place. One hundred yards into the path, there was one of those little stems. He picked it up and Charlotte held out her hands so David placed it gently on the palm. They continued to walk. Between every five paving slabs another one of those little stems grew. David continued to pick them and place them into Charlotte's hands. They reached the end of the alleyway, blocked by a solid brick wall. Charlotte turned and looked him dead in the eye, smiled softly and whispered, "run".

David opened his eyes with a start. The TV was still on but the film had finished and now there was a man with far too much makeup on trying to sell him a special tool that helped to fillet fish. David looked at the clock, it was a quarter past midnight. He had been asleep for more than eight hours yet he still felt tired. It was very warm so he cranked the window, downed his flat Bud and stripped to his boxer shorts before walking to the toilet for a piss. He flushed and took a step over to the sink to wash his hands.

He was greeted by a drawn dark-eyed face in the mirror. "Christ" he said "I'm glad I don't have to be in work until ten". He turned rubbing his eyes and walked out of the bathroom, failing to notice the two protruding spikes appearing from beneath his arm.

+++

Charlotte had been ringing all morning but there had been no answer. Also, she had received no responses to her text messages and now she was beginning to worry. It was very unlike David not to answer, maybe he was unhappy about her missing their DVD night. Still, she expected at least some sort of response, just something to let her know he was okay. Charlotte decided that if she heard nothing before lunch, she would walk round the corner to the garage where he worked.

"Are you coming down the cafe, Charlotte?" Jessie already had her purse in hand and was standing by the office door tapping on her mobile.

Charlotte looked up from her computer screen, "I'll meet you down there, I've just got to pop over to the garage" she said.

"Still no reply then?"

"No," Charlotte laughed, "bastard." There was, however, a hint of unease in her voice.

Logging her computer off, she left the small office and the door shut softly behind her as she walked into the busy street outside. There was no air and as she walked, her pale pink shirt clung to her chest and stomach, vacuum packing her body in a sticky wetness. Charlotte heard car horns and revving engines from the nearby city centre, the heat of the afternoon making tempers rise. As she walked, she tried to phone David but it once again rang through to voicemail. She didn't leave a message.

Charlotte rounded the corner and could see the garage, shimmering like a mirage in the distance. She reached it in two short minutes and walked in, straight up to the till. Stephanie was sitting behind the counter reading some sickly romance novel with a shirtless man on the front.

"Hey Steph, could you give David a shout for me please?"

"Little shit, didn't turn up for work today" replied Stephanie, "hence I get woken up at 10:30 on my day off to come and cover for him." She looked up from her book. "I thought you must have pulled a skive with him for a bit of late morning sex!"

"No," Charlotte looked confused, "No, I haven't spoken to him."

Charlotte left the garage at a slightly quicker pace than she came in, and started heading to the apartments David lived at. On the way she text Jessie, letting her know that she may be back a bit late, and to cover for her. She tried David again, still no response, so for the third or fourth time she left a message after the beep. As she walked purposefully past tall buildings, housing multi million pound businesses, past what felt like hundreds of newsagents called things like 'Choudhry's' and 'Deepak's', past people holding out free papers and others trying to sell expensive ones, she kept her hand outstretched to hail a taxi. One stopped just outside 'Gupta's Off Licence' and she jumped in.

The taxi ride took five minutes and cost £7.50. Charlotte jumped out and jogged towards the main door to the four storey apartment block. She pushed the buzzer to call David's intercom and waited thirty seconds. No answer. She tried again and waited another few seconds. Each floor held two apartments, one north facing and one south. The lift, which Charlotte had never seen out of order, ran up the centre.

David had lived in his apartment for just under four years now and Charlotte had been with him for three, so why, she wondered, had she not introduced herself to the neighbours? Charlotte tried each of the apartment buzzers and got two answers. One was an elderly lady from apartment 1A who wouldn't let Charlotte in without ID, and before the man who answered the 3A intercom could speak, he was dragged away by a giggling female.

She was wondering what to do next when the postman came out of the lift with his royal blue satchel over his shoulder and walked towards her. He opened and held the door for her as she walked in. She walked past him and straight into the lift, selecting the fourth floor.

As the lift rose, Charlotte looked at her reflection in one of the three mirrored walls. She could see the worried look on her face. She was worried that David had hurt himself and was lying dead on the floor or worried that David had decided that he didn't want to be with her anymore. She didn't know which was worse. The lift came to a slow stop with a ring and a mechanical voice announcing the destination reached. The doors opened immediately and Charlotte walked out, her heels tap tapping on the grey tiled floor. She reached the door to David's apartment and lifted her hand to the brass knocker just above the letter box. Before she could knock the unlocked door began to open.

+++

*In the early hours of that morning, after David's marathon sleepathon, he was struggling to sleep again despite feeling utterly exhausted. The light from the streetlamps two floors below his window cast a glow from the top of his curtains. He had lain awake for what felt like hours just staring blankly at the ceiling; his eyes following swirls in the Artex. Lifting his hands to the top of his head, linking his fingers, he stretched. He felt like shit; had never felt this* tired, this drained. He twisted his body to the side, taking up as much of the wide bed as possible, tousling up the duvet beneath him. Then something caught his eye - a cobweb, a thin strand that ran across the room from the deep red lampshade and into the corner where a thick funnel like web attached itself to the coving. He could have sworn that it hadn't been there earlier but just assumed it was a quick working spider. It wasn't large, maybe four by three inches wide and a solid white in colour. David propped himself up onto one elbow and glanced around the room; vision starting to blur as the night continued to take its toll; but he couldn't see the webs lodger. Not to worry, he thought, even his thoughts were beginning to slur, I'll find you in the morning. He chuckled out loud; or was it in his head; as he slipped gently into delicious sleep.

  David woke up suddenly, a few beads of glistening sweat had sprung up on his forehead, a scream only just held inside his lips. He had experienced the dream again. It had begun the same, the walk down the paved alley, solid walls either side, the same plants every four or five steps. It had changed as they had reached the end of the alley with the daunting red brick wall blocking their path. Charlotte had turned to him, her hands cupped in front of her, full of the round leafed weeds and it had actually been Charlotte this time, not just a dream interpretation of her. This time, however, she didn't say "run". In one swift motion, she dropped the plants to the floor and grabbed the sides of his face. David had instinctively grabbed her wrists but he couldn't move them. His eyes looked towards the floor, the stems seemed to be rooting back into the ground and spreading towards his feet. He tried to move them away but his feet were stuck to the paved floor with some sort of invisible force. The weeds moved onto his shoes and up underneath the hem of his trousers. He could feel them sticking into his legs, bare beneath his chinos. They felt like tiny mosquito bites but deeper. Beads of blood dripped gently down his legs. Now Charlotte spoke, although it was nothing that David could understand as the English language, more of a guttural, tribal cry.

*As she did, a second set of arms ripped from her torso, spraying blood in little rivulets that the weeds seemed to lean towards, and tore into David's chest. Long, jagged fingernails scraped though skin and muscle, boring a deep hole inside him, her fingers curling around his ribs. Then she jumped high, landing on the wall amidst the sound of bones breaking and flesh tearing...*

*Before David had woke, he had seen the thick trail of webbing that she had left behind.*

*David rubbed his eyes furiously, "stupid". He said this aloud, the voice sounding strange in the dark, making him feel even more stupid than he already did. He realised, of course, that the dream had been caused by that damn spider's web that still sat in the corner of his room. He glanced at the clock on his bedside cabinet; a Jack Daniels alarm clock that his Aunt Kate had bought for him a couple of Christmases ago. The little hand was halfway between the three and the four. Despite the early hour, David had already decided that his friend, Henry the Hoover would shortly be evicting the arachnid from its stolen home.*

*He pulled the duvet off his chest, throwing it to one side and pulled his elbows up on to the bumpy mattress, half sitting up. He stopped, a confused frown on his face and slowly moved his hands towards his body, fingers reaching out. There was something there, laying each side of him. He moved the thumb of his left hand over something hard, rutted and thin. He did the same with his right hand, suddenly feeling very cold. His palm grasped the foreign object in his bed. He quickly pulled both hands away, falling back onto his pillow. Not only could he feel the gnarled sticks lying adjacent to his semi naked body but he could feel himself feeling them. He launched himself out of the bed, duvet falling to the floor, and hit the mahogany cupboard shoulder first, ignoring the bolt of pain that shot up his neck. Panic hit him, the sane part of his mind telling him to calm down, that it was only a dream. He didn't quite dare to flip the light switch, wasn't ready to look just yet. All the same, he needed to know.*

"From this day on," David spoke in short gasps, "I will stamp on every fucking spider I see".

He reached across his body, his right bicep grazing against a scab-like roughness and put his finger to his left armpit. The gash had gone; it had been filled up with whatever was growing out of him.

+++

David heard the buzzer going off, heard his girlfriend's voice as she talked to Mrs Draping from downstairs. He heard the giggling couple from directly beneath him, both through the floor and as the sound came through the window from the entrance doors intercom. She couldn't get upstairs to him. He stood strong, didn't go to the window to look out at her.

Then, there was the postman. David heard the click of the heavy wooden door, the cheery voice of one of Her Majesty's servants and soon enough the loud merry ring of the elevator reaching his floor. The click of stilettoed shoes moved towards his apartment, getting louder on the wooden floor. He heard her raise the knocker on his front door. No, that was wrong. He *felt* her raise the knocker. Felt her grip and felt the door slowly begin to open.

+++

The door only opened a few inches at first and Charlotte could smell something that didn't belong there. An earthy, mouldy smell, like a fungus, and it was strong. Charlotte squinted and wrinkled up her nose as she pushed the door further with her foot and the smell hit her with an even greater severity. It wasn't just that earthy smell, there was something else, something rotting, festering. It smelt, almost, like death.

"David?" she called, "baby? Are you in here?" Charlotte pushed the door fully open, peering in to the hallway, barely lit even with the afternoon sun. She breathed through her mouth to keep the smell from entering her nostrils but she could still taste it. She gagged, glad immediately that she hadn't yet had her lunch. Turning her head she had to will her accelerated breathing to return to normal and she pushed the cramp in her belly away.

Charlotte had to find out if David was okay, realising with that thought that she loved him, more than anything. She turned back to the open door and cautiously stepped over the threshold into the apartment. Two steps in and the air seemed to change. It became cooler and the smell less fetid. There were sounds too, movement surrounding her. Only soft, but enough to send a shiver up her spine. Charlotte reached her hand towards the light switch, found it and pushed the button. Her pupils contracted as soon as the light hit them and she realised how dark it had been.

She blinked her eyes, overwhelmed by the bright light, floaters momentarily blocking her vision. Her hands instinctively rose to her face, rubbing away the strange shapes. She pulled her lower eyelids down, looking up and then blinking, refocusing on the scene in front of her. She was too shocked to do anything but shake her head, not understanding the scene in front of her. On the floor, the carpet was alive, moving. It was covered with weeds, bright green, round leaved and each plant about ten inches long. The walls were almost totally with a thin patchy green-black moss, pale tendrils that seemed to reach out towards her. She looked up. Hundreds of long legged, spiderly creatures moved between hanging, twisted vines, along thick strands of newly sewn web. Millions of eyes staring straight at her. Suddenly and at the same time every spider let go of the funnel web or their leafy vine. With a simultaneous hiss they fell quickly to the floor, their inch long legs tucked in to their swollen, black bodies. They opened up as they hit, the full four and five inch bodies sprinting towards their target. Charlotte couldn't suppress her scream this time, she turned back to the door but it had noiselessly shut behind her.

She grabbed for the handle, ripping through the vines that grew thickly there. She screamed again as she felt the long legged arachnids touch the skin beneath her trousers. She screamed as they crawled from the thick overgrowth down her fingers and up her arms, disappearing into her shirt. She screamed as she furiously slapped at her stomach to stop the creeping, hooked legs moving over her; the things exploding like balloons of creamy white pus. They held on to her hair even as she relentlessly shook her head backwards and forwards in violent disbelief. She kept screaming until the creatures found her open mouth.

+++

David looked down at the corpse of his former lover, watching the pitted skin shift and stir, moved by the creatures climbing her bones. He watched through closed eyes. He watched through the multiple eyes of the spider like creatures, the ones that still crawled from blinking, breathing holes in his hardened skin. He could see as their hooked feet pulled at the ravaged flesh from the inside of the rapidly disappearing bag that once housed the soul of Charlotte Ellen Maille.

David could feel his subconscious stretching out as the vines grew down from the ceiling, spreading dark leaves across the walls. He could feel them using the energy they had taken from the dead woman on the floor, growing, reaching out, meeting the round leafed stems on the floor, intertwining, as if they were holding hands. The whole apartment seemed to beat in rhythm with David's heart and every throb sent a shimmer across the floor.

Light from the hall still filtered faintly through the thickening foliage and the moving leaves on the floor sent flashes across the walls like a jungle rave. David couldn't help but think of the lines "Hush my darling, don't fear my darling. The lion sleeps tonight". He tried to laugh but nothing more than a scraping, dry rasp emerged from the small hardened slit where his mouth had been. He stood in the living area between the mossy sofa and widescreen, high definition TV, unmoving, surrounded by mouldy photos in cracked glass frames held at impossible angles by twisted leafy stems.

He heard the loud, merry ring of the elevator reaching his floor. He heard the voice of Mrs Draping enquiring as to the scream she had heard from downstairs. He felt the brass knocker of his front door being raised up. His door began to open as the hall light stopped shining through.

+++

Jeanie skipped around the corner, trying to keep up with her brother "You're 'spose ta walk me home from school Jakey, slow down".

He had slowed down, in fact, had stopped in the middle of the pavement. She almost bumped right into him. Jake was staring straight ahead, open mouthed. Jeanie peered around his leg to see the blinking lights of both a police car and a fire engine. There were a number of people standing around, most with the same expression as her big brother. They were all staring at the green mass in front of them.

"Jakey", Jeanie said, looking up at him and tugging at his trouser leg, "why is everyone looking at a bush?"

Jake didn't speak, just took her hand as they walked across the road. Jeanie looked confused as they stopped just outside of the short wooden fence, the same wooden fence that had, this morning, circled round where she lived. It wasn't a bush that everyone was looking at; this was her 'partments'. Jeanie stared at the leaves covering the building that had been bright, clean and white before she had left for school. They flashed blue and white and yellow in time with the turning lamps on top of the vehicles in front of them.

Jeanie thought how pretty it all looked. She thought how pretty it looked until she saw the hundreds of eyes staring out at her, each one an individual flashing ball. Everyone else appeared to notice this at the same time because it became almost silent, just the low hum of the vehicles and the distant drone of faraway streets.

Jeanie let out a small squeak as she saw a giant spider creeping towards her; it was as big as her head! Jake had seen it too and he took a step forward, stamping down on the arachnid with a sickening squelch. Thick white jelly oozed from beneath his black plimsoll. The instant his foot hit the floor a deep, dark, other worldly sound came from the building. That sound caused almost everyone to shiver, hair standing up on the backs of the necks.

David lifted the curtain of vines from what used to be the main doors and walked slowly outside. He limped along on legs which were too thin, his trousers viciously torn in places showed the ripped, gnarled flesh. He must have been in pain but what was left of his face gave nothing away. The lower jaw hung at an awkward angle from what could have been a thin tendon but looked more like a bloody vine. His left eye was black and swollen, weeping thick viscous fluid down a split cheek. His right eye was missing, in its place a woody stem. His hair still looked fine.

The shout of fear and disgust from the still growing crowd was very obvious and most took an involuntary step back. One of the police officers, a female in her mid-twenties, took a few step forwards, towards the obviously wounded man, ready to help or to run. It would turn out to be neither.

She began to say, "are you okay?" when the man, David, stopped and let out a loud rattling cry.

It could not have come from his mouth, which no longer existed but it did come from him. He lifted his arms, tearing the shirt from his yellow withered body and as he did, revealed the two new arms which grew from beneath his own. They stretched out, unfolding and pulled his body backwards, the rattling growing louder. His legs began to crack open releasing two more new limbs which anchored into the ground. The upper limbs had pulled his body into something resembling a giant, wrinkled mouse foetus. This all happened in less than thirty seconds. The policewoman had drawn her baton.

Most of the crowd stood and stared, both loving and hating the freak show which took place in front of them. It was what happened next which caused them to move. The body of David began to split.

The tear began at his groin, slowly at first and then speeding up as his skin ripped all the way to his throat with a sound like ripping paper. The two halves flapped over like a popped balloon. This is when the spiders leapt from the building, running towards the crowd in a blanket of black.

Almost everyone who had been there died on that first attack. It was only Jake and Jeanie who saw the rest of the show. It was only Jake and Jeanie who saw the swarm of anthropomorphic creatures pulling themselves from the belly of the man in front of their home. Only Jake and Jeanie who saw the spiders turn from their feasts and run towards the creatures emerging from the broken body of David, covering them with their hundreds of legs, embedding into blue-green flesh, creating a living armour. Only Jake and Jeanie saw the creature's standing in a line before the vine covered building; wide muscular bodies with thick necks and angular heads; before they began to march forwards in unison, weapons held at their chests. It was only Jake and Jeanie who looked straight into the creatures eyes; oval, expressionless purple swirls. It was only Jake and Jeanie who saw the rest of the show, and it was the last thing that they ever saw.

## Spiders

My room was full of spiders
When I woke up in this morn,
One million tiny mirrored eyes
All looked at me with scorn.

I felt them crawling on my toes,
A web adorned the wall,
My weary eyes could see them
As they walked into the hall.

I swung my feet onto the floor,
Minding where I stood,
They cowered from my footsteps
As they tapped on splintered wood.

I pulled upon my trousers;

A faded pair of jeans,

Magenta on the pocket,

Mem'ries from fading scenes.


Their fangs were sparkling crazily,

Light from the waning moon,

It breached the parted curtains

Outside my mother's room.


I reached towards the door knob,

Softly called her name,

"Mummy, it's the spiders,

They're driving me insane."

No movement from the silent bed,

The duvet humped quite high

And something dripped onto the floor

Then I began to cry.


My sobs and moans then turned to screams,

I shot up in my bed,

But no-one ran to comfort me

And everything was red.

## The Wall

"Do you not understand it Dweedlebum?" Muntun Fitsqueal asked.

"Of course I understand it," Dweedlebum answered, glaring at the fat man in the pink suit. "I just don't understand what purpose it serves in this case."

"I think it is perfectly obvious," squawked the second head of Muntun Fitsqueal as he poked inside his ear with a long bony finger.

Muntun Fitsqueal's second head was one of those heads which really pissed people off. Of course, the first head of Muntun Fitsqueal hadn't planned it that way but after paying out 150,000 Jalbeerian dollars to a spermapod for the upgrade, there was no way he would admit to other people that he was not happy with it.

"Well?" Dweedlebum said, still glaring.

"Oh you do look odd, is that a new hair cut?" Muntun Fitsqueal's second head said.

Dweedlebum turned away. As his eyes swept past the wording on the wall above the console he saw it change.

"A mimica," he gasped.

"Very clever," squawked the second head of Muntun Fitsqueal, although he seemed a bit dismayed.

The first head of Muntun Fitsqueal just mumbled.

"What is a mimica?" Titti VonTrapp was still standing in the corner watching him work. Dweedlebum had almost forgotten.

"A mimica, my dear Titti, is a mask." Dweedlebum turned to make sure that she was watching. "It is a rumour which stops you from understanding the truth. However," he beckoned the pretty Swanarian Princess forwards, "if you find the correct angle, you are able to see the truth behind the lie."

She gasped, a gorgeous sound that would have turned the head of every humanoid in the room, if they had not already been looking directly at her.

"I see it," she said and beamed, revealing pearly white teeth.

"I am very glad," Dweedlebum said and gave her a little pat on the bottom as he walked past, towards the console.

"I don't know why you worry so much about tiny things like this," Muntun Fitsqueal's second head said. "I mean, it's not as if anything he has ever written has come true."

"Are you sure about that?" Finally the original head of Muntun Fitsqueal spoke up, turning towards the head sharing the patch between his left and right shoulder.

"Of course I am."

"Do you mean?" Muntun Fitsqueal began. "Are you saying?" Muntun Fitsqueal continued. "That I am aware of something that you are not?"

"You do know that is a scientific impossibility, don't you?" the second head of Muntun Fitsqueal said but his voice had taken on a shaky quality.

"Because," Muntun Fitsqueal carried on, a broad smile appearing across his heavily jowled face, "if that is the case then I am entitled to either a replacement upgrade or a removal and a full refund."

"Well what is it that you think you know that I don't know, with the knowledge that I know everything that you know and many things you don't?"

"Well, I'm not likely to tell you that am I, because then you will know what I know and you would deny not knowing it until I decided to tell you."

"I would never…"

Dweedlebum thought it was very likely that he would. He had been very good friends with Muntun Fitsqueal before the upgrade had been performed and he decided that he would enjoy watching the removal. He wondered if the spermapod surgeon would reposition Muntun Fitsqueal's original head during the operation or if that would be an additional expense. If so, judging by the recent finances of the pink suited fat man, he would likely be sporting a sideways glance for a rather long time.

Dweedlebum turned to Titti VonTrapp and smiled.

"Shall we make a move?" he said.

"What about the...?" She flicked one hand at the writing on the wall above the console.

He turned and regarded the dark red words.

"No, I think those two will be arguing for hours, then of course there is the Argentium Space Fruit to dissect. You would just get bored."

"Where too then?" She looped her arm in his and they walked out, tails flapping in the wind.

## **Dick**

      Walter's Tavern is quiet for a Saturday night. In fact, it has as much life as a cemetery. There are three guys over in the corner in the booth nearest the bar, staring at nothing, each cradling a cloudy drink in a chipped glass. One of the guys I think I recognise, though I can't be sure. Then there's the dog curled up by the bar which is empty except for a couple of frayed beer towels and some rancid peanuts. How do I know they're rancid? They're the reason our jolly bartender, Clyde, had his teeth knocked out yesterday evening by a couple of cats who hadn't liked the taste. He isn't much of a conversationalist; he can barely manage a grunt.

      I look into the dark amber of my drink, watch it through the ice cubes that I hadn't asked for, but had been given anyway. I like the way the light shines through it, moving shapes across the scratched and dirty table. I like the way it looks, it helps me think, to evaluate whatever case I'm working on. I never take a sip though. Not a drop of hard liquor has passed my lips since 1939; cross my heart man, hope to die.

Gently, I push the tumbler across the table where it catches on a deep gouge and almost tips over. I watch it for a second – the liquid caressing the surface of the glass – before I turn and stand to face my coat, which hangs on a hook by the door, underneath a sign marked 'Hats'. My own hat is still on my head, pitched slightly forward, hiding my eyes. I take a step forward and the door opens, a soft wind rocking the unshaded bulb hanging between me and the exit. I look up at the silhouette snaking towards me, the perfect hour glass figure, all hips and bust, hair bouncing off her shoulders in time with the click, click of high heels on a tiled floor. I touch the lip of my hat as she passes me, but any reaction is lost in the shadows. I let out a breath that I didn't realise I'd been holding and walk towards the door, reaching for my pressed beige overcoat. My hand hovers in the stale air when I hear the woman's voice.

"Any messages?" A husky voice, a southern twang that I'd know anywhere.

I turn slightly to the left and glance over my shoulder. Clyde was in mid head shake – no messages. I consider turning and calling her name, but think better of it. I unhook my coat and swing it over my shoulder.

"You not even gonna say hello?" That voice again, that sweet, dangerous voice.

I turn, resigned to my fate. Emerald green eyes framed with fiery red hair.

"Red Winters," I say.

"Dick Harris," she says. She smiles as she says it. I fell in love with that smile, a long, long time ago.

We look at each other for a long second, until Clyde places a glass onto the bar beside Red. Me and her look towards it at the same time. Red reaches over and runs one fingernail up the slender stem before reaching the bowl. I watch as her fingers caress the curve, drawing lines through the water mark. I feel a droplet of sweat run down the side of my face and she reaches up to it. Her fingertip so cold, yet so soft that I barely feel it. She pulls back, touching her finger to her mouth, leaving a shine on her bottom lip. I lick my own lip instinctively.

"You still off the hard stuff?"

I blink and shake my head slightly, returning to my senses. "Sorry?" I say.

"Liquor," she lifts her glass up to her lips. "Still not drinking?"

"Cross my heart and hope to die," I say, drawing an X across my chest.

"Do you want a coffee?"

"Don't think they do coffee here." I glance at Clyde; his swollen, broken lips form a silent O as he shakes his head.

"I've got coffee upstairs, handsome."

"You live here?" I'm not surprised, not really. Red living in a dirty bar in downtown New York was something I should have expected. What does surprise me, though, is that why, in all the bars in all the towns in all the world, did I have to walk into hers?

She places her glass back down on the bar and turns. I'm powerless to stop myself and I feel my feet move. I see Clyde – a towel in one hand, a glass tumbler in the other – a strange little smile on his face. I ignore him and my mind starts to catch up with my feet.

I haven't seen Red in nearly three years and I haven't thought about her for a long time. We were tight for a while, too tight for her 'cause she split one night. Took my money and my gun and pulled the old disappearing act. I looked for her of course; used a few good contacts who owed me favours. I stopped when I realised it had all been for the best. After all, I'm a private dick, she's a hooker. Sounds more like a Hollywood movie than real life. I can picture it now: 'Dick, The Private Dick' starring Dick Harris and Nancy 'Red' Winters. Sounds like a kick.

I walk through the narrow doorway and glance at Red as she moves up the stairs. Her pale calves smooth beneath a deep green dress, the cotton tight around firm thighs. Her buttocks move beneath the material as if they were trying to escape from their confines, and shit, did it look as if they were having fun trying.

I lose sight of her for a moment as she turns right at the top of the stairs. When I reach the carpeted corridor she's waiting for me outside the first door. She pulls at a silver chain around her neck and everything inside me tells me to turn on my heels and get out before I'm sucked too far in. A small silver key struggles out from between the swell of her breasts and my thoughts of the cool air outside disappear. I fleetingly wonder how she manages to keep those girls from popping out, but then she unlocks the door, takes my hand and leads me inside.

+++

Red slips from beside me and stands, her body lithe as a serpent and pale as a ghost. She is mesmerising and my eyes focus on a bead of sweat just south of her right buttock. I watch it travel down her leg, kissing her skin until it stops behind her knee. She walks away and into the dark bathroom, closing the door behind her and I hear the shower turn on.

I sigh, but I'm not sure whether it is one of happiness or of angst. I mean, she is the perfect woman and she knows how to please her man, but I've been her man before and I know the other side of that coin. I silently curse myself as I realise that I let her seduce me again, and so easily. Have I got no mind of my own? But is it really my fault? Maybe I've never lost that flame for her; after all it wasn't me who had extinguished the fire, it was her. It was her who had walked away; it was her who had run. She hadn't even left a note, no sign that she wasn't happy. Why the hell was I up here?

The water stops and the door opens, releasing a cloud of bitter-smelling steam. Red stands in the doorway, embraced by a black velvet gown. Her striking eyes sparkle through strands of wet hair.

I stand, facing away from her and pull my underwear and pants on. They don't feel good over my damp, sticky body and I feel dirtier than a whore on Diamond Street, which is pretty apt. I pull at my belt as I scan the floor for my shirt, but look up as a hand rests on my shoulder.

"What have you been up to then, Dick?"

I turn to her. She's kneeling on the bed, the skirt of her gown riding up seductively high, the collar slipping dangerously low. I could see in her eyes that she knew she'd done wrong; maybe this was some sort of an apology.

"Where you been, Red?" I say, ignoring her question as I pull a slightly crumpled packet of Marlboro from my pocket.

She doesn't answer, just takes the cigarette I've just put in my mouth and places it between her own curved lips. I take another from the pack and then offer her a match before lighting my own. I watch her draw smoke in before letting her hand drop, closing her eyes and letting it out again. She doesn't release her breath, just lets the grey mist spiral up from her lips. I used to like the way she smoked, but now, she was just another broad with another dirty habit.

We're both silent for a while. She keeps looking at me and I keep avoiding her gaze. She walks back into the bathroom and I find my shirt, still wishing for that coffee.

+++

Business hasn't picked up by the time I walk past the smiling Clyde. It looks like the three deadbeats in the corner have been reduced to two. The one I recognised has disappeared. The dog hasn't moved an inch; I'm not sure it's even breathing. I take a last look and walk towards the exit.

As I reach for the door, it opens and a large man blocks my way. I sigh, look up at him and smile.

+++

It was 1942 and I was working a job on Cannery Row, at a little biological testing site called the PBT. A woman's body had been found out the back by the specimen tanks. The poor broad's head was no longer attached to her neck, but had been located. It had been pickled in a glass jar and hanging suspended in the porch of the home she shared with her husband and four year old daughter. The first thing her husband had seen as he walked out that morning was the blue face of his wife, mouth open in a silent scream.

I was still a cop back then, an investigator with delusions of grandeur. I was young, I was naïve and Ritchie Hartman was my only suspect. Hartman was a small time gangster; petty stuff, you know. Crimes you wouldn't write home about; minor drug dealing; small time shoplifting, that kind of thing. It was common knowledge that he was a womaniser, an up and coming athlete and a good-looking man. The dead woman, a girl called Betty Richards, had been seen with Hartman a few times in the weeks before her death, so naturally...

Maybe she'd tried to end the relationship? Maybe he'd seen her with someone else? Maybe he'd got drunk and made a mistake? Maybe he'd finally snapped? There were a lot of questions, a lot of maybes, but that was all I needed. I knew it was him and I gave him hell. Hartman had a rock-tight alibi, but what does that matter to a twenty something cop with his eyes set on a detective badge? I trailed him, day and night, pestered him constantly; pestered him so much that he'd drawn a gun on me. I shot first.

Only, he hadn't drawn a gun; he didn't have a gun. He had a photo, a photo of the man who had killed Betty Richards. I lost my badge, but he has never lost his limp.

+++

He kind of sneers at me, not a look that I'm unfamiliar with in my line of work, before offering me his hand. I take it and give it one solid shake – all business.

"Ritchie Hartman," I say. "I see they've been feeding you well down in old Monterey." I gesture with my chin down to the gut protruding above his belt.

"Remember, Dick," he says in his twenty-a-day voice, "you're not a cop now and I always keep my blade handy."

I look up at him in time to see his scowl turn into a smile and he grabs my shoulders, pulling me into a hug. There aren't many guys who I'd let hug me, but damn he's strong!

"Let me buy you a drink, old friend," he says, releasing me from the bear hug. "I've been looking for you everywhere."

"You know what?" I say, "let's go somewhere else, I need a cup of coffee." I know that behind me, Clyde is rolling his eyes.

+++

We settle on a well-lit café on Broome Street; a red and white sign hanging outside advertises it as 'Bongo's'. I order a coffee from a pretty middle-aged waitress in a pristine white apron; Ritchie goes for steak and fries. As we wait for our order I just look at him. There is definitely something on his mind. Not sure I've ever seen him looking so detached.

A different waitress brings our order over and Ritchie ploughs in. I lift the coffee to my lips but it is far too hot, so I push it to the side of the table and lean back, watching the food on Ritchie's plate swiftly disappear.

"You said you'd been looking for me," I say.

"Hm?" He looks up from the half masticated cow. "I've got a job for you."

I consider this for a moment. Ritchie has never offered me work before. Why would he? He has his own men, men with a lot less inhibitions than me. He tosses his cutlery down by the side of his smeared plate.

"My kid came home the other day—"

"Little Robert, how is he?" I ask.

"He's good. He came home the –"

"How old is he now?" I ask.

"Seven."

He waits a moment, looking at me before continuing.

"He came home the other day and told me something." He lowers his voice, close to a whisper. "He said that someone had... you know?"

"Hit him?"

"No."

"Mugged him?"

"No."

"Run over his dog?"

"For fuck's sake, no!" he says, shocking me. I've heard him swear before, but never with ladies present. "Someone, touched him... you know?"

"Sick f—"

"More coffee sweetheart?" The first waitress appears again. I look up at Ritchie who is draining the last of my coffee. He shakes his head and waves her off.

"I need you to... talk, to the guy who done it," he says.

There is only one reason I can think of that Ritchie hasn't already nailed this guy to the door.

I nod to him. "What's his name?"

He looks at me with an expression that's a cross between a pained frown and an angry grimace and says the name that I'm expecting. "Father Edgar Songs," he says.

His brother-in-law.

Before I leave, Ritchie slides a sheet of paper across the table. It says 'Meet contact 10am, wear a disguise'. There's an address at the bottom.

+++

It's not easy to find a specialist costume shop before 9am on a Sunday morning, even in the Big Apple; unless, that is, you know where to look.

My outfit is slightly snugger-fitting in places where I would prefer it not be snug, but to an untrained eye, it's passable. I smooth the creases out of the thin fabric as I walk towards the corner of Nassau Avenue and Henry Street, opposite the church. I kinda like the respect I get dressed as a nun and smile at the people who bow their heads as I pass them. Ritchie told me where I would meet my contact and I'm quite pleased to see that the man in front of me must have studied at the same school of undercover investigation techniques as me; he's dressed as a priest. A stiff, three peaked biretta rests almost jauntily on the top of his head and he's wearing an obviously fake, bushy black beard. His collar is a dazzling white and his cloak's so dark that it makes my tunic look almost grey in comparison.

I nod a small greeting. "Father," I say, attempting to heighten the pitch of my voice for the benefit of the sparse human traffic.

He nods in return, but eyes me a bit warily. Nice acting – you never know who's trying to set you up.

"Is he in there?" I gesture at the large church, its windows dark.

He pauses and looked at me with dark, narrowing eyes. "I'm sorry, Sister?"

I think for a second, trying to remember if Ritchie had given me a code word. When I look up, the priest has taken a few steps away.

"Hey," I forget about trying to disguise my voice and a few stragglers turn their heads. "Ritchie didn't give me a code word."

He looks at me, eyes widening over his nylon face fur. "Ritchie?" There is a slight tremor in the word.

"Yeah," I say. "Ritchie Hartman."

With that, he turns and runs. It takes me more than a few ticks to realise my mistake and I hitch up my skirts, revealing pulled-up black socks and hairy legs. Before I even get close to the fleeing man, a 1954 Lincoln Capri, sky blue, screeches up to the kerb and the priest runs headlong into it. A woman jumps out as the front wheel scrapes the edge of the sidewalk. She grabs him, knocking that damn biretta off and chucks him, without ceremony, into the rear of the car. It's only then that I realise I've stopped running and am standing in the middle of the road, skirts still hitched up above my knees, staring at the most beautiful woman I've ever seen.

"Get in, Dick," she says, breaking my reverie.

She jumps back into the driver's seat and guns the engine, further snapping me out of whatever daydream I'm stuck in. Whoever the hell this beautiful broad is, she means business. I run towards the front of the car, jump and begin sliding across the bonnet Gary Cooper Style, a smug look on my face. My feet touch the floor on the other side just as my trailing habit snags on the hood ornament pulling me into a kind of tuck and roll. My feet kick out, my habit rips and I head-butt the bonnet before sliding to the floor.

+++

The woman doesn't do a great job of concealing the glee that she has written all over her face as I manage to pull myself into the front passenger seat of the Lincoln. She looks at me, smiles, then hands me a handkerchief that looks as if it may have been used on at least two previous occasions.

"You're bleeding," she says to me as she pulls out in front of a cursing cyclist.

I look at her side on. She's blonde, real blonde not out of a bottle, or so I can tell with my limited experience with hair colorants and her eyes are blue, sparkling like sapphires. She has a short, straight nose that tilts up a touch at the end and her lips are thin and perfect. I inadvertently compare her to the woman I spent the previous afternoon with and inwardly sigh, not for the first time. I dab at the graze on my head and it comes away with a light spattering of deep red.

"So, who the hell are you?" I glance at the gun shaped bulge beneath her belt before remembering my contact sitting silent in the back seat. I turn to him; he's staring out the window, a look of fear on his face.

"Ritchie didn't mention me?" she asks.

I must have looked confused.

"You've already met the Father, I see."

Then the light dawns and I look back again. "You mean that beard's real?" I say.

Father Edgar Songs opens his mouth to reply, but the woman beats him to it.

"You fucking open your mouth, I'll cut your tongue out," she says.

I like this woman, she speaks her mind, she doesn't hold back.

"Nice costume, by the way," she says, with a smile that only makes me feel a little bit stupid.

I realise I don't recognise the street we're on, which is strange 'cause I know this city like the back of my hand. She pulls down a long gravel drive and stops just short of a set of rusty gates at the entrance to a long-disused warehouse. There is a sign nailed up above the shutter doors directly behind the gates, but there are too many letters missing for me to recognise the name. The fencing to either side of us is cracked and broken and someone had scrawled something unreadable across one of the panels in black paint. She opens the door and steps out, so I follow her lead and look at her across the Lincoln's roof. The sun is strong, bouncing off the roof and I find myself squinting, so I can't quite see her.

"So, who are you?"

"Ritchie thought we might get along," the woman smiles.

"And what do you think?"

"You look okay, but your dress sense leaves a lot to be desired."

I can't tell if she's serious or not.

"I normally have a bit more notice when I'm meeting with a woman," I say.

Her blurry shape nods and she moves around to the front of the car. As she comes into view and I blink away the black spots floating in front of my eyes, she raises her hand.

"I'm Lois Love."

I take her hand, it's small and cold. "Dick Harris," I say, "but I guess you already knew that."

"Of course," she says. "Dick Harris – recovering alcoholic, failed police officer turned expert private investigator, never carries a loaded gun."

"Ritchie tell you that?" I ask and she nods. I realise I'm still holding her hand and I relax my fingers and drop mine to my side. I look at her for a moment, examine her face. There is a small scar just above her right eye and I realise absently that I want to kiss the place where someone had hurt her many years previous.

She breaks the silence. "You don't have any questions for me?"

"Ahh, Miss Love – failed marriage, unhealthy obsession with candle wax and a dark past in tic-tac-toe." I enjoy the look of incredulity on her beautiful face.

"How did you—?"

"Miss Love," I say, "remember, I'm a private investigator."

She chuckles at that as she walks past me, opens the rear door and drags Father Edgar Songs out onto the stony ground.

+++

The gates are unlocked and I push them open. A creak that sounds extraordinarily loud in the quiet sends a few birds flying from the trees surrounding the drive. We walk up to the large green shutter doors, me in front and Miss Love behind, dragging the priest by the beard. I'm still shocked that it doesn't come off with the ping of elastic at every sharp tug she gives it. The door looks as if it would collapse inwards with a solid kick but Miss Love produces a key from a pocket of her jacket and unlocks a shiny new padlock, which looks out of place in the rusty metal ring, before sliding the shutter up.

I look into the large open space in front of me, full of shadows, and hear Miss Love flick a switch. After a couple of sputtering instants the warehouse floor is filled with light and I can see what we have to work with. The floor is empty apart from a sturdy-looking chair in its centre. A coiled rope sits on the seat. The priest must have seen it too, 'cause he starts to whine and I turn to see him squirming.

"Hold on to him," Miss Love says to me and I walk over, grabbing the priest's dog collar with a firm grip.

Miss Love walks back to the shutter door and pulls it closed which somehow makes the room look brighter.

"Who are you, what do you want," the priest stutters, wide eyes looking straight into mine.

I am about to answer when Miss Love reaches an arm around him and puts a gleaming blade to his throat.

"Now, what did I say about talking, Edgar?" she says and Edgar stops moving.

I take my hand away and Miss Love leads him towards the chair, knife still against the bearded skin of his throat. I follow and pick up the rope just before she pushes him down on to the chair.

"Do you know how to tie a rope?" she asks.

"I know how to tie my laces," I answer.

I'm not used to this. I find that a few well-meaning threats normally do the job but it seems Miss Love has other things on her mind.

"Hold this," she says, gesturing towards the knife.

I take it and she makes a show of lashing the rope around the man, binding his arms, hands and torso to the chair. She nods at me and I take the knife away. I notice a small droplet of blood that wasn't there before I took the knife. Miss Love must have seen the sliver of panic in my eyes 'cause she turns and takes my arm.

"You can wait outside if you want. Ritchie asked me to deal with this in a certain way and said that you might not feel comfortable with it."

I nod, but stay where I am. As nervous as I am about seeing whatever Miss Love is going to do, the way she moves around the seated, bound man, the way she touches his shoulder from behind and whispers in his ear, the way she smiles at me, all make me want to stay. That, and the knowledge that this man in front of me, this man of God, touched Ritchie's son in a way that no man should ever touch a child.

"Are you staying?" she asks and I am enthralled by the sparkle in her sapphire eyes. She takes my non-answer as affirmation and says, "wait with him for a second."

As she walks past me, the camomile smell of her morning shampoo wafts into my nose and I breathe deeply, eyes closed, before I know what I'm doing. I hear the shutter door roll up and sunlight spills in, causing shadows to shoot across the floor. I look at Edgar Songs. His eyes are red and tears are falling down his cheeks.

"Please," he says to me, failing to keep his voice steady, "let me go."

"No can do, Father," I say but I begin to feel sorry for him.

"What are you going to do to me?"

I don't have time to answer as I hear the shutter doors close behind me. I turn and Miss Love walks towards me holding a bag. She walks past me and drops the bag with a clang at the priest's feet.

"Who are you?" he says, grunting between sobbing breaths.

"I ask the questions," she says as she crouches and unzips the bag. She pulls out a gag and hangs it in front of his face between a slender finger and thumb. "How many little children have you violated?" Her voice is steady, sweet, loving almost.

"None," he says with an obvious effort.

She draws her hand back and whips the gag across his face, the buckle leaving a welt that is immediately obvious. He squeals and tries to pull away from her but the chair doesn't even move. I notice for the first time that it is bolted to the floor.

"How many have you touched?" she says.

He doesn't answer this time and gets the same treatment. The buckle of the gag strap hits him in almost the same place and a thin rivulet of blood appears on his cheek. I see him muttering something under his breath and realise that it is a prayer.

"Your God won't help you now," Miss Love says with a snarl and pushes the gag into his mouth, buckling the strap behind his shaking head.

+++

I walk from the warehouse in a haze of confusion and awe, only to find two large men standing between our car and a small black van with 'S.E PAINTER – Pest Eradication Experts' stencilled on the side. Miss Love's small hand touches my arm and I turn to her.

"Don't worry, Dick, they're with us."

I look into those bright eyes and realise that I was falling for her; falling for this small gentle woman, a woman who could somehow perform the atrocities that I had seen in the warehouse behind me. I have never before witnessed a body being taken apart with such ease, with such happiness as had happened in there, and yet, despite that, I want to take her slender frame in my arms and touch my lips to hers.

It had been almost beautiful to watch her work. It hadn't taken long for the priest to tell us all about the sick acts he had performed on countless children and I stopped feeling sorry for him in short order.

She had begun with the fingers and ended with the eyes.

I turn back to the men, where they stand, behind the van, rear doors now open, pulling on white overalls. Miss Love walks over to them through the open gates and I watch her, enjoying the way her bottom moves at each step. She talks briefly to the smallest one and then turns to me.

"You coming?" she asks.

"Sure," I say with a smile. "Where to?"

"Your place. You need to get some decent clothes on."

+++

Ritchie had arranged for a theatre trip that evening to see the Broadway revival of Finians Rainbow. Why he thought a production about a penniless leprechaun would be of any interest to me was beyond my understanding but Miss Love seems excited and I want to be in on the ride.

The streets are busy on the way to my apartment; it is nearly six and the sun is warm and bright. We slow down a few blocks away and pull into an empty parking lot.

"Be back in a moment," she says, pulling up the hand brake.

I stay in the car and watch as she enters a nondescript building and disappears. I assume she wants to wash up. She had worn gloves throughout most of the act of 'pest eradication', but a red stain tinged her fingertips. I don't have to wait long.

Miss Love emerges from the building through the same door she had entered, in a black figure hugging dress that leaves little to the imagination. She knows I'm watching – it would have been hard not to notice the childish maw of my mouth and my wide eyes – and she plays up to the fact that she looks more than good. I wish I could hold that tight body in my arms.

+++

We reach my apartment less than ten minutes after leaving the lot and I'm upstairs and back outside within five. We reach the theatre at half past six, thirty minutes before curtain up. I wonder if they serve coffee here.

The place is packed out, which makes me slightly uncomfortable. I work on my own, not because I'm unsociable, but because I'm just not keen on the majority of society so when I see people looking at me in shock and overhear them whispering to their friends and wondering how I get to be next to the beautiful woman by my side, that just gets my goat.

It takes us a while to find our seats in the theatre with very little help from a pre-pubescent usher with far too much Brylcreen slicking his hair back underneath a little red hat. We do eventually manage to locate them and settle down between an old couple and a man with liquor on his breath.

Miss Love seems enthralled by the whole thing, from curtain up to curtain down; and grips my hand during a song in Act II by Sharon McLonergan and Woody Mahoney. I'm not going to lie and say that I enjoy the performance quite as much as Miss Love but I'm actually surprised to find myself humming along with a few of the songs.

"Wanna cry, wanna croon,

Wanna laugh like a loon,

It's that Old Devil Moon

In your eyes."

There is a standing ovation, which I guess is less due to my monotone humming and more for the performance in front of us. There are three encores (three!) and Miss Love claps and cheers as loudly as everyone else. When the lights shine on, the crowd begin to leave. I prod the drunk man next to me with an elbow, shocking him awake. He stands and nods thanks before bidding Miss Love a farewell and walking up the aisle. I stand and make to follow but Miss Love takes my hand. I'm hoping for a romantic walk beneath the stars and possibly a goodnight kiss but she sits me back down instead.

"Ritchie got us backstage passes," she says. "I know a couple of the actors, I'll introduce you."

I smile at her and she kisses me, full and long. She tastes of peppermint ice cream with chocolate sauce and I relish every mouthful.

+++

When the place has all but cleared out we make our way down the aisle to the front and knock on a door to the side. A burly security guard opens it and we show our passes. Walking into a stuffy room Miss Love begins to look around for her actor friends while I feign interest in the large selection of stage props on a table in front of the doors to the dressing rooms.

"Isaac," she calls out, her hand waving almost frantically above her head.

She runs over and jumps into the arms of a topless man with the body of a god and a face to match. I follow in her footsteps, but without the frivolity and without the leap. I try to hold the eyes of the man with my girl on his bare chest.

"Dick, this is my good friend," Miss Love says over the wide shoulders of the superman in front of me. "This is Isaac."

He releases his arms and Miss Love drops to the floor. I grab his offered hand and squeeze, watching his face for any sign that the bones in his hand are beginning to break, but there's nothing. I find myself getting a little jealous, then he speaks.

"Hello, Dick, wewy pleased to meet you."

He has a shockingly girly voice and his r's roll quicker than the traffic on the New York State Thruway. I have to stifle a grin.

"Wewy... I mean very, pleased to meet you," I say. He doesn't seem to notice my error.

"How long have you been intewested in acting?" he asks and I decide to play along.

"Acting? Oh, ever since I was a kid." Isaac smiles at this. "I was actually in a play recently, a modern one called 'The Hands of Song'."

Miss Love gives me a wary glance but I see that there is still a twinkle in her eye.

"Ooo, I haven't heawd of that one."

"James!"

I turn and see Miss Love's backside rocking its beautiful way towards a short balding man in a blue tweed jacket. That's better, no competition. She throws her arms around his neck.

"Why don't I show you awound?" Isaac asks in that near perfect representation of Mickey Mouse.

"That'd be nice," I say and I think I even sound a little bit interested. Maybe I should have a serious think about this acting gig. "You got any coffee?"

He sends a young girl off with a flutter of one loose hand without asking how I take it. Not that I mind how it comes, not this late in the day.

The chiselled statue of a man leads me off towards the dressing room doors as Miss Love and the one she calls James, head out to the stage in the opposite direction. The dressing rooms are compact but look comfortable, albeit a bit messy with a sickening array of colourful garments draped over gold-rimmed mirrors and shiny glass lamps. Short-backed chairs sit in front of tiny tables where a number of half-dressed broads sit in front of their own reflections, removing stage makeup as swiftly as they reapply their own thick disguise. If it was still Saturday evening I would have struggled to draw my eyes away from this amount of supple female flesh, but all I can think of now is Miss Love; her peppermint kiss had really taken my breath away.

"This is ow dwessing woom," Isaac says, stating the obvious.

He isn't much of a guide and turns back towards the door without introducing me to anyone. I follow and we walk out to find a steaming coffee on a flowery tray, and the glowing face of Miss Love with a smile just for me.

"Do you mind if I borrow him for a moment, Isaac?" she says.

He looks a bit upset at losing me mid-tour, but he agrees with a sullen nod. I walk over and take Miss Loves hand. She leads me towards the stage and away from my drink, her fingers slipping between mine and holding on tight.

"Isaac seems nice," I say.

"He is," she agrees. "I've known him for years."

We walk out on to the stage. It's a pretty incredible sight; the auditorium is empty and the lights are low. There was a green carpet spread across the floor. Who needed a starlit walk when you had fake grass and fluorescents? She stops walking and turns, adjusting her grip on my hand. She looks me in the eyes and I look straight back into hers. Then, that kiss again, that beautiful kiss from those beautiful lips. Ritchie Hartman, you wonderful man.

The kiss is over far too soon and I still have my eyes closed as she runs her smooth finger over my right cheek. I lick my lips.

"That was wonderful, Dick."

I nod and that's when everything goes black.

+++

I open my eyes and have to close them again as my pupils dilate in the furious light from above.

"He's awake," someone calls out; a woman's voice – middle aged, local.

I open my eyes again into a squint and look around. I'm lying in the middle of the stage and I can feel the plastic bristles of the carpet scratching at my pants. I glance to my left at the prop bag that had fallen from the rafters and landed on my head. It had 'PENNIES' stencilled on it in thick black lettering.

My head hurts like hell so I reach up with my left hand and rub. There's a bump the size of a baseball and it feels wet. I draw back my hand as I wince, then I remember.

"Miss Love," I say, "where is she?"

"Lois?"

"Yeah, Lois," I say as I try and sit up.

"Just stay there, Dick. We alweady called the cops."

I sit up quickly, ignoring the bolt of pain that shoots though my brain and grab the rhotacistic giant by the collar. "Where the fuck is Lois?" I say.

"We d-d-don't know, Mr D-D-Dick."

Great, a stutter too.

"S-s-someone dwagged her wout."

"Who?" I say as I realise I'm still holding the shirt of the shaking man. I release him.

"We d-d-don't know. They were gone b-before we weached them."

I have to get out of here before the cops arrive. They know me well and there's no doubt in my mind that they'd play with me in an interview room for a few hours. By then, Lois's trail may have cooled and I'd be stuck. I try to stand. My legs won't obey at first, but then I'm up and walking towards the exit.

+++

I really don't know where to start. I know nothing of Miss Love's life; no friends, no relatives. I go to the only person I know has had any contact with her. First stop, Ritchie Hartman.

Ritchie lives in the rough end of town; a scrape off the shoes of any well-meaning New Yorker. I find that I spend a lot of my time in his neck of the woods, but familiarity doesn't breed admiration. I think there's a saying somewhere along those lines.

Ritchie's a gangster and that makes him difficult to get close to. Even if I do manage an audience with him, I often find that he's not quite himself. He plays a role in company; much like Isaac but without the flowers. It doesn't help that his men all know about my shady past as a cop. Cops, even ex-cops, and gang members don't seem to mix too well. Still, I have to try; Ritchie may be the only person with any leads.

I arrive outside of the laundrette that I know is the face of Ritchie's empire. I've always thought a laundrette as a stupid place for any criminal organisation to reside. After all, what gangster flick doesn't have a laundrette somewhere in its play? I walk in to the sound of a bell which is hanging above the door. There's a short Asian woman behind the counter, almost blending in with the smartly pressed suits and freshly washed shirts hanging behind her.

"I need to speak with Ritchie," I say.

"I no speak Engrish," she says.

"You said that in English," I say with the sweetest smile I can manage.

"I no speak Engrish," she says.

I've played this game before. "Listen," I say, speaking as slowly as I can. "If you don't get Ritchie out here, there will be more than lipstick stains to remove from those suits." I keep the smile on my lips. I find that a threat with a smile makes it all the more believable.

"I no speak Engrish," she says.

This is going to be harder than anticipated. I reach into the inside pocket of my jacket, slowly, keeping my eyes fixed on the little woman in front of me. It's a risky move but I'm hoping she'll back down rather than reaching behind the counter and picking up a loaded shotgun.

Three men, roughly the same size as bulldozers, careen through the wall of shirts sending empty coat hangers crashing down onto the hard tile floor. The lead guy, an ugly brute who appears to have been on the wrong side of a hammer on more than a few occasions, points a gun directly between my eyes. I slowly remove my hand and drop it to my waist.

"Who the hell do you think you are?" His voice sounds like boots on gravel.

I look back over my shoulder before returning my gaze to him. "Me?" I ask as my finger touches the centre of my chest and my left eyebrow lifts.

"There ain't no one else here," the second guy speaks up with more sand than gravel.

He's no prettier than his companion but at least he has good hair.

"Is Ritchie about?" I ask.

"Answer the question," the third one speaks and completes the circle; the three stooges, the three musketeers; the three little pigs.

"Dick Harris," I say. "I'm a friend of Ritchie's."

They all look as if waiting for the other to speak and then gravel throat steps forward with malice in his eyes. I hear the phone ring from somewhere in the room as he throws his first punch. I dodge to my left, shrugging my shoulder down as his massive fist grazes my right ear. I hook my arm around his and twist, pulling him off balance before smashing my left knee into his rotund stomach. He pulls a shallow breath in and his legs crumple beneath him. I stand straight again before the other two trolls step forward.

"Stan' down boys." We all stare towards 'Speak no Engrish'. She puts the phone down on its cradle and says, "he fren' with Ritchie."

"Told you so," I smile.

"Rot a bruddy mess," she says as she looks at the crumpled clothes on the floor.

I walk behind the counter, and stepping over the heap of jackets follow 'Speak no Engrish' into a dimly lit corridor.

"Rait here," she says before walking to the door at the end, knocking and walking through.

I waited for nearly fifteen minutes.

"Dick," Ritchie says from behind a wide mahogany desk, "don't ever come in here like that again."

I look at him, eyes wide with disbelief.

"This is a place of business, my business, and I don't appreciate people coming in and making a damn mess."

I can't believe he's talking to me like this, but then I notice the dark silhouette of a man in each corner of the room behind him. He's making sure they know he's boss in his own house.

"She's been kidnapped, Ritchie."

"Who has?"

"Lois," I say.

"She's a big girl," he says. "She can look after herself."

"I need to know where I can find her, Ritchie."

"How am I supposed to know, Dick? Look, give me half hour and I can get you another broad. What do you want? Blonde? Brunette? Fat? Thin?"

"Ritchie, please," I say, "you owe me one."

Ritchie stands up at that and I think there is real anger in his eyes.

"I owe you nothing. You're still paying me back for shooting me."

"I thought I just had," I say.

"Nowhere near, Dick. Songs was a favour, but Lois done most of the work."

I can't believe what I'm hearing. Not only is he refusing to take Miss Love's kidnap seriously but he's berating me for my assistance in the Father Edgar Songs case. There is something he's not telling me.

"Do you know anything about Lois?" I ask.

"What are you saying, Dick?"

"I'm saying nothing, Ritchie," I nearly spit out his name. "Do you know where she is? Where she lives? Any of her friends? Anything about her?"

"Is she really worth the trouble, Dick?"

"More than worth it. I've got to go."

I turn and walk out. The argument had been going nowhere and it had been getting there fast. I think, if I hadn't have walked away when I had, in the gunfight that would have followed, someone would have ended up dead. Not holding a weapon myself, I'm guessing it would have been me.

+++

I could think of only one place to go, so I head back towards the theatre in the hopes that the cops had taken their statements and headed to the closest doughnut shop.

I hop from the cab I had waved down just under thirty two minutes before. As I do, I see the last of the cruisers pull away from the kerb. Waiting until it is just out of sight, I walk to the door I had exited earlier that evening and knock as there is no external handle. It opens almost instantly.

"Dick!" Isaac stands in front of me, almost filling the doorway. "Have you found her?"

I ignore the question. "Who has access to the stage props?" I ask.

"Evewyone." His whining voice is beginning to annoy me.

"Get everyone together; I need to speak with them."

"Most people have left alweady," he says and there is no small amount of fear in his eyes.

"Well," I'm close to shouting, "get everyone who's still here."

To give him his due, I came to be in front of a group of fifteen people within ten minutes. I look at them all, hoping that my super PI sense would tell me something; it doesn't. I clear my throat and am about to speak when a kid, no more than eighteen, walks in, yawning.

"Who are you," I say.

The boy tries to speak, but I've caught him mid yawn.

"This is Kelvin," says Isaac. "He's our pwop boy."

The boy suddenly looks scared.

"The rest of you can go," I say, "thanks for your time." The group begin to peel off. Isaac doesn't move. "You too, Isaac."

He looks a little upset, but moves off without another word.

"What's happened?" the boy asks before stifling another yawn.

He's as white as vanilla ice cream.

"I want to speak with you about the abduction."

"Abduction?" he asks and uncertainty moves across his face like a cloud.

"Yeah, the abduction."

"What? Here?" Getting information from 'Speak no Engrish' had been easier than this.

"Of course here," I say. "Have you been asleep?"

"Yes," he shocks me with his response. "It wasn't my fault though," he says. "This woman—"

"What woman?" I fight the urge to grab his shirt and shake the answers from him.

"I dunno, just... a woman."

"What did she look like?"

"Blonde," he says, "great breasts. We was getting on really well and she asks to see the props and stuff, so I brought her back here. I thought I was gonna get lucky, ya know?"

"Was this before or after tonight's show?"

"Before."

"Carry on."

"Not much more to say. She was really flirty, you know? Kept pushing her boobs out at me, like this." He pushes his chest towards me, as if I wouldn't understand. "Then, when I asked her what her name was, she stuck me with this."

He holds out his hand. In it, is a syringe, quarter filled with a clear liquid. I take it from him and hold it above my head, examining it against the light. I can see that, in fact, it is not quite clear; it clouds under the fluorescent with a blue tinge. There's only one person who can tell me what this is; I need to visit The Doctor.

+++

Just over an hour after I arrive at the office belonging to The Doctor, he steps back to me, syringe in one hand and notepad in the other. He's not really a doctor, of course, not in the traditional sense of the word. He has no medical degree or any legal experience with patients, yet ever since the case of the missing sapphire three years back, he is the person who I always go to with problems of this nature.

"What have you found, Doc?" I ask as he places the syringe on a table covered with papers.

He's a white haired man of about sixty and wears tiny spectacles on the end of a long straight nose.

"Nothing that could be of any help I doubt," he says in a broad German accent.

"Why don't you let me decide that?" I say, in a far blunter tone than I meant.

"Of course, Dick. But first…"

I hand him a thick brown envelope, which he pushes unopened into a pocket in the back of his brown corduroy trousers.

"This is a rather common barbiturate called pentobarbital. It is a sedative and can, in some places, be bought over the counter. It comes as a salty powder but it's soluble. Fast acting, very effective for short periods."

"You say it can be bought over the counter?"

"When I say over the counter, I don't mean in a pharmacy. Prescription yes, but anything else, you have to know where to find it."

"And where could I find it?"

The Doctor turns to his desk and picks up a pen. He writes on his pad, tears the page off and hands it over. I look at it and turn towards the door.

"You won't find anything out tonight, Dick. There'll be no one there and they have two rather nasty Chihuahuas guarding the store room."

I sigh.

"Go get some rest, Dick. I'm sure whatever you're working on can wait a night."

"I hope so, Doc. I really do."

I walk from the offices and hear the locks turning behind me. I look at the address on the paper The Doctor had handed me. There is something that I'm forgetting, or just not realising. I decide to take a walk, think about things in the cool air.

I see a light on in a distant building and can hear the faint sounds of music coming from within. I head towards it. The closer I get, the more the address eats at my subconscious. Where have I heard it before? The sound of the music grows closer. I find myself on the same street I had left so unhappily on Saturday evening and then I work out why I know the address. I walk further down the street and approach Walters Tavern. I glance at the address above the door and then to the building next door. There are four evil eyes and two sets of sharp teeth bared through the window.

I take a moment, a second to breathe the night air in, then pull my eyes away from the nasty-looking Chihuahuas and push open the door to the bar.

It's far busier than it had been on my last visit. Clyde still stands behind the bar and I'm not even sure he's changed his clothes. I nod at him and he smiles back.

"Jack Daniels, straight," I say, before adding, "no ice." He turns his back on me and dips a glass tumbler into an ice bucket.

"Hiya handsome." I knew she'd be down, but I couldn't have guessed it would be so quick. "I knew you'd be back."

I feel a hand brush my shoulder and hot wet lips touch my cheek.

"Look, Red," I say, but she cuts me off.

"Is it because of my job?"

Maybe my guess is way off or maybe she's a better actor than Isaac could ever be.

"No," I say, "nothing like that."

"'Cause I can leave it. We can get married. I can learn how to sew."

"Red—"

"Don't say it, Dick. I love you so much."

"No, you don't Red."

The wonder leaves her eyes for a moment and it's replaced by anger. She looks as if she may slap me. "Is it 'cause of that bitch, Lois Love?"

Got ya. "Where is she?" I ask.

"Let's talk upstairs," she says, "away from prying eyes and flapping ears."

She stands and I stand too. Clyde, I notice, has walked around the bar and is keeping an annoyingly close distance.

"Don't worry, Clyde. He's not going to hurt me," she says. "Are you, Dick?"

She doesn't wait for a response, just turns and walks towards the door. I follow her and Clyde follows me.

+++

"Don't mind Clyde, he's very protective over me."

"Where's Lois?"

"I know you kissed, I watched it happen."

I glare at her.

"Where's Lois?" I ask again.

She shrugs her shoulders and a smile plays on her lips.

"Where is she?"

"Clyde, would you go and fetch her?"

Clyde doesn't say a word, but looks at me.

"Don't worry. Dick won't try anything stupid."

He didn't seem to like the idea, but began to walk towards the door.

"Wait," Red says, stopping him in his tracks. "I think me and Dick here need to make a little deal." She turns to me. "How much do you want her back?"

I don't answer. My face must have told her everything she needed to know.

"Here's the deal, Dick. You're mine and you've always been mine. I've watched you for a long time and I know you feel the same."

This broad is fucking insane.

"We can leave here and never look back. I promise you, your precious Lois will be set free, completely unharmed."

"No deal."

"What's the alternative, Dick? What choice do you have?"

She's right. What choice do I have? I either agree to go with her and trust the lying psycho will let Miss Love go, or I try and get her out without getting myself and her killed.

"I need a guarantee," I say.

"Don't you trust me, Dick?"

I laugh at the very suggestion.

"Very well," she says with a smile. "Take off your clothes."

"What? No." I'm surprised to see her laughing.

"She sees you with another woman, she runs out crying. You watch her leave. She gets on with her life, finds Mr Right and has a long and happy life."

I fail to see how that would possibly happen. After all, she had already seen me get knocked unconscious and been dragged kicking and screaming to a locked room somewhere on the top floor of the bar. Sometimes, there's no reasoning with a psychopath. I nod at her and she nods at Clyde, who removes himself from the room.

"Why is he helping you?" I ask as I begin to loosen my shirt.

She ignores me and lies on the bed, undoing the buttons down the front of her dress. I see her naked flesh again and something inside stirs. This time it isn't lust, its disgust. She pulls me on top of her and our skin touches. She moans loudly and kisses my closed lips. I can taste wine on the tip of her tongue as it pushes between my ungiving lips. I hear footsteps from the corridor outside the room and she grabs my hair, turning my head towards the open doorway. She moans again and arches her back, pushing me up. I see Miss Love walk past with Clyde on her right. She turns, she sees me, and her face drops.

I can't stand it and I leap from Red, running across the floor. I make it through the door and straight into Clyde, who grabs my face and smashes it into the wall.

+++

My right eye opens and I look around the room. The thought that I have been unconscious more often than not in the last 24 hours crosses my mind and I realise that I still haven't had my coffee. I'm no longer in the hallway; I lay on my side on the worn carpet at the window side of the bed, facing the wall. I sit up quickly, head spinning, then sniff, tasting blood at the back of my throat.

"You're awake my darling." Red sits on the side of the bed, facing away from me, long legs hanging over the side. "I thought you'd be asleep for hours, Clyde gave you a hell of a crack."

"Where's Lois?" I ask, my voice dry and nasal.

She turns to me like something from a horror flick. "Where's Lois? Where's Lois? She is nowhere! She is nothing! You are mine, forget about Lois!"

"Where... Is... Lois?"

She turns back, anger gone as quickly as it had surfaced. "She's right here, Dick."

I force myself up, pushing against the bed and look past Red. Lois is tied to a chair, a gag in her mouth, a deep cut across the side of her face. Clyde stands to her left with a short blade in his hand.

"Let her go," I say as I drop to my knees. "Just let her go. I'll do what you want."

I watch Red stand and walk to Lois. She raises one hand and strokes the unmarked side of her face. Lois tries to pull away but Clyde grabs the back of her head so her eyes are on her abductor.

"She is beautiful, Dick, you made a good choice."

I can't look at her, my eyes are on the floor and I'm defeated.

"Cut her," she says and my head shoots up.

"What?"

"Cut her. Then I'll let her leave."

"What?" I ask again.

"The way I see it, Dick, you take away her looks, you take away her appeal. You're a man, Dick, and I make it my business to know how a man thinks." There's a loud bang from downstairs but neither Red nor Clyde seem to notice, "and men, they're all as shallow as each another."

I look at her, unbelieving.

"No? Shame. Clyde, do you want to do the honours?"

"No," I scream out. "Wait." Red looks at me in anticipation. "I'll do it," and Red's smile grows as she licks her lips.

"Your knife, Clyde." Clyde hands it over as I rise up and walk around to the other side of the bed. Before Red hands me the knife, she says "and don't think you can do anything without having to get past Clyde."

I look at Clyde, who stares at me through blackened eyes and smiles with his broken, swollen lips. He's built like an ox. I nod at Red and she hands me the knife. I walk over to Miss Love, but can't meet her eyes.

"No, Dick," Red says. "From behind. I want to see you do it."

I close my eyes, sigh and walk around the chair, standing behind Miss Love and in front of Clyde. Red looks intently at the knife as I sigh again.

"In your own time, Dick," she says.

There's no time like the present. I tighten my grip on the knife then swing my arm round in an upwards arc. My eyes are nearly closed, but I feel the blade slide through the flesh of Clyde's throat as if it were butter; I feel warm wetness spray my face and run down my arm as my hand begins to slip from the handle; I feel Clyde's massive hand move the air in front of my face and I feel the bullet from Red's gun hit me in the back, even before I hear the gunshot. I pitch forwards and my face hits the hard floor in front of the dying man, whose blood is beginning to pool beneath his horizontal frame. My vision swims but before blackness sweeps me under I hear two more gunshots and I know my love is dead.

+++

Blurry, inconsistent, phantom figures walk around me.

Voices, everywhere, all around. No sense of time. No sense of space.

Numb. Eyes being opened. Blinding light.

Burning pain.

I try to reach behind me to the ache in my back but my arms won't work. I try again, harder, forcing out a moan that seems to sap my strength.

Voices again. Footsteps.

Then nothing.

+++

I wake in a panic and take a furious breath in. I am in a dark room. There are no sounds but a constant mechanical beep. I roll my head to the side and see Miss Love, sleeping in a chair beside me.

+++

Three days pass before I'm able to keep my eyes open and my mind alert enough to question the whereabouts of Miss Love.

"She's been with you day and night for a little over a week, Mr Harris." The plump brunette in the nurse's garb leans over me, her ample bosom pushing into my side. "She's just popped downstairs for a coffee with a friend of yours."

Lois walks in at that moment and the nurse steps back just in time to avoid being trampled. She kisses me and I feel tears spring up in my eyes. I savour the moment before looking up towards the door and at Ritchie Hartman.

"What happened?" I say to Lois, but keep my eyes on Ritchie. "Where's Red?"

"Reds dead," she says and I catch her smile from the corner of my eye.

"Why is *he* here?"

"He saved me."

Ritchie steps forwards and hands me a steaming cup of coffee, so I sit up, leaning backwards against uncomfortable pillows. "Sorry about Sunday," he says. "Turns out that a few of my men weren't as loyal as they should have been."

I think back to the meeting with Ritchie, of the faceless men standing in the corners of his room. "Red?"

"Yeah, and the barman."

"I'm sorry, Ritchie. I should have trusted you."

"Well, I didn't want you to know they were in there with me." He chuckles, but there's no humour in it.

I notice that he'd said he didn't want me to know. Not that he'd had a gun pointed at his back or there'd been a gun pointed at me. He just didn't want me to know. I take a long sip of the bitter coffee and relax back against the pillows, eyes closed, before placing the cup on the trolley beside my bed. I look again at Lois and see that she has taken a few steps backward and now stands beside Ritchie.

"You know what they say, Dick," Ritchie continues. "Never let a hooker do a hitmans job – they're both good with a bang but one has too much breast and not enough brain."

He takes Lois's hand and I'm lost for words.

"You shouldn't have shot me, Dick," he says, shaking his head slowly back and forth. "You shouldn't have shot me."

"Ritchie?" I'm confused, though I shouldn't be. I don't know what he's saying, yet I know exactly what he's saying. "But that was a million years ago."

"I was destined for the stars back then, Dick. One shot from some motherfucking cop on a power trip, and the world came crashing down."

"You know I'm sorry for that, Ritchie," I say, "I've told you enough times." I take the coffee from the trolley.

"Not as sorry as I was, Dick." He lifts his wrist to his chest and checks his watch. I gave him that watch.

Lois smiles over at me and I'm pretty sure there's pity in her eyes.

"Red didn't want to do it, you know?" she says. "Ritchie paid her a lot of money, but after she took me into that dive tavern of hers, she told me she'd changed her mind, said she still loved you."

A migraine starts to build behind my eyes and by the feel of it, it's gonna be a doozy.

"Course," Ritchie steps back in, "Chase was with us all along, keeping an eye on things."

Chase Montgomery! I knew I'd recognised that guy in the bar. I go to take another sip of my coffee but I can't lift my arm. It's strange, but I don't really care and my pains have gone.

"Red shot me." My voice comes out quietly, my mouth dry. "Why'd she shoot me if she still loved me?"

"You killed her brother," Lois says.

"Clyde?" I cough, clear my throat and start again. "Clyde was Reds brother?"

Neither Lois or Ritchie answer me. I try to speak again but my vocal chords seem uninterested in obeying. A nurse walks in behind Ritchie and Lois, but I can't tell if she's the same one from before. The world has taken on a shimmering quality, as if it's wrapped in cellophane and I can't quite focus. I glance down at the coffee cup, held at a slight angle in my limp hand and understand now, what they have done, what they must have delivered to me in that dark, oily brew.

"We better be off now, Dick," Ritchie says from far away.

I try to move, try to get the nurses attention but I'm so tired; I've never been so tired. I think I see the nurse walk out again but I can't be sure. Lois comes into view and leans in close. I can feel her warm breath against my cheek and the soft scent of camomile arouses what senses I still have left. She kisses my lips, gently, beautifully, before moving to my ear.

"Enjoy your coffee," she says.

Writing for children as Tony Gilbert –

Super Fred

The Cloud Diary

Published by Visionary Press:

Doodeedoo

Published by Ghostly Publishing:

The Youngest Knight (to be released early 2015)

Featured in anthologies:

No Sleeves and Short Dresses (as Tony Gilbert)

A World of Terror (as Tony Gilbert)

Terror Train (as A. P. Gilbert)

Printed in Great Britain
by Amazon